BEWARE OF THE DOG!

Boo!

Joe Fenton

SIMON & SCHUSTER BOOKS FOR YOUNG READERS
New York   London   Toronto   Sydney

For Dulcie and Ken

SIMON & SCHUSTER BOOKS FOR YOUNG READERS
An imprint of Simon & Schuster Children's Publishing Division
1230 Avenue of the Americas, New York, New York 10020
Copyright © 2010 by Joe Fenton
SIMON & SCHUSTER BOOKS FOR YOUNG READERS is a trademark of Simon & Schuster, Inc.
For information about special discounts for bulk purchases, please contact Simon & Schuster
Special Sales at 1-866-506-1949 or business@simonandschuster.com.
The Simon & Schuster Speakers Bureau can bring authors to your live event.
For more information or to book an event, contact the Simon & Schuster Speakers Bureau at
1-866-248-3049 or visit our website at www.simonspeakers.com.
Book design by Laurent Linn
The text for this book is set in Bikini Bottom Redux.
The illustrations for this book are rendered in oil paints.
Manufactured in China · 1109 SCP
2 4 6 8 10 9 7 5 3 1
Library of Congress Cataloging-in-Publication Data
Fenton, Joe.
Boo! / Joe Fenton. —1st ed.
p. cm.
Summary: A ghost tries to find a way to scare
the other ghosts in his family.
ISBN 978-1-4169-7936-4
[1. Ghosts—Fiction.] 1. Title.   PZ7.F351Bo 2010   [E]—dc22
2009017768

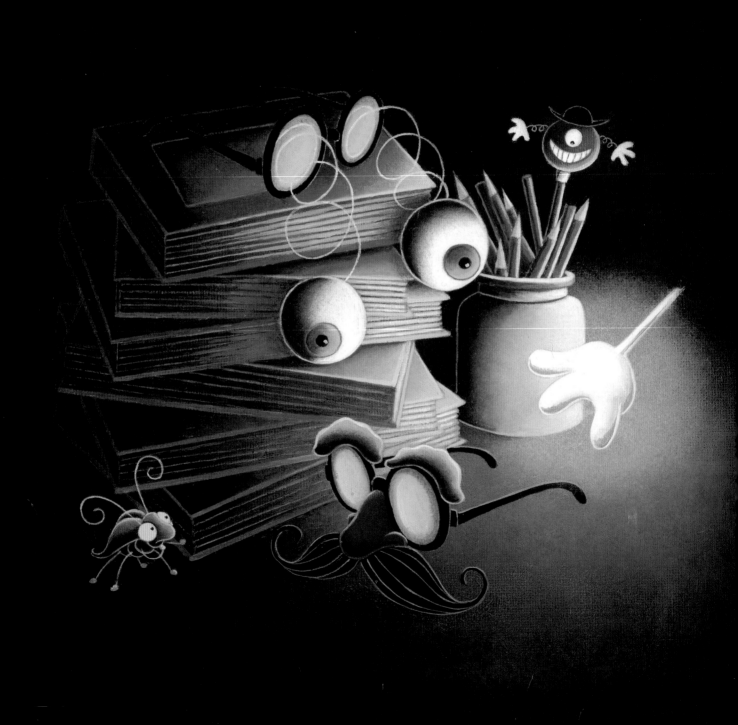

SCARY THINGS

FrankenStein

GLOW
PAINT

BLACK
PAINT

FRANKENSTEIN

Booo

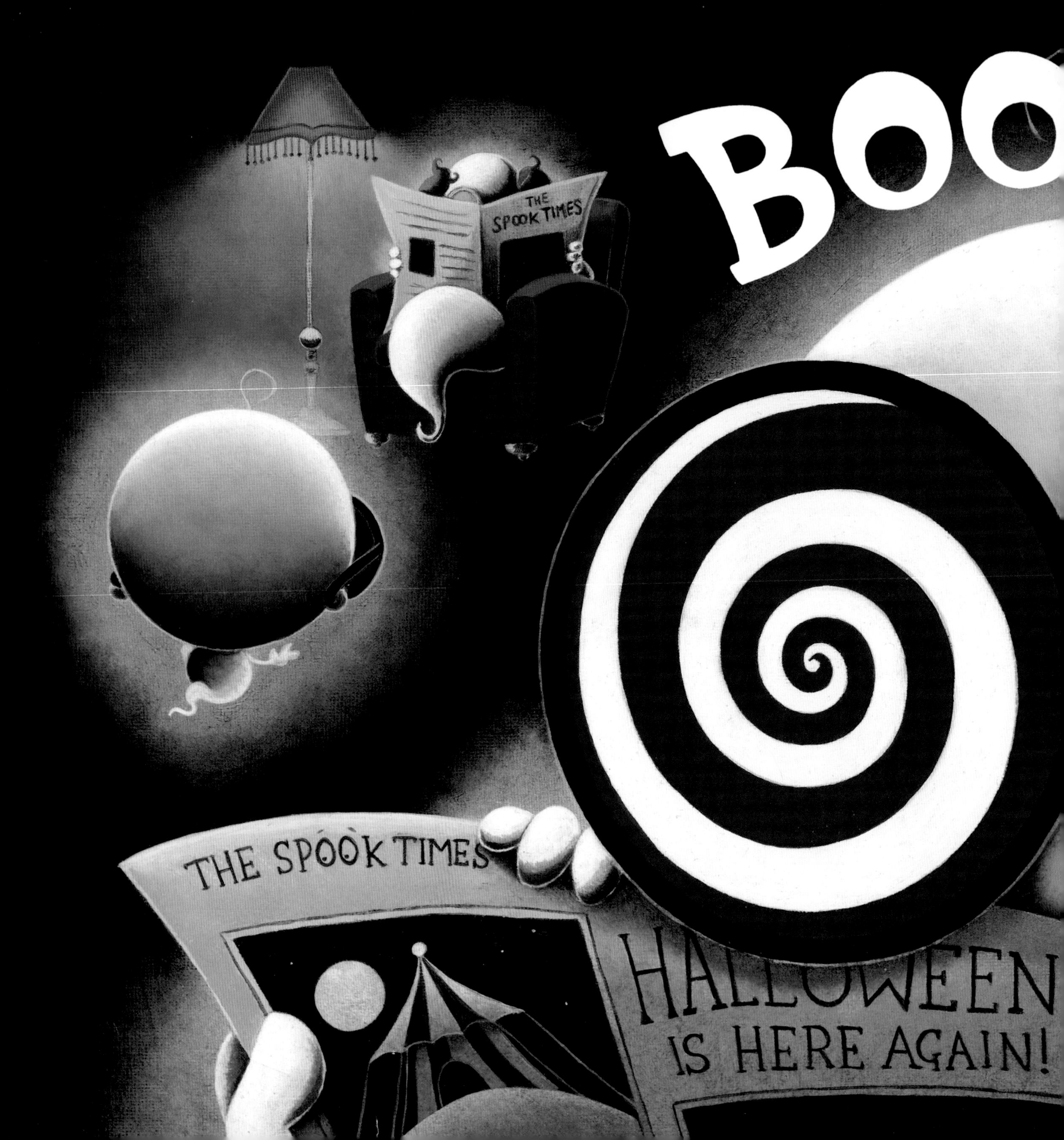
BOO
THE SPOOK TIMES
THE SPOOK TIMES
HALLOWEEN IS HERE AGAIN!